J F Wooden, John A2447
Wooden, John R.
Adventure underground

ADVENTURE UNDERGROUND

by Coach John Wooden

with Steve Jamison
and Bonnie Graves

Illustrated by
Susan F. Cornelison

Perfection Learning®

Editorial Director:	Susan C. Thies
Design Director:	Randy Messer
Cover Design:	Tobi Cunningham

For information, contact
Perfection Learning® Corporation
1000 North Second Avenue, P.O. Box 500
Logan, Iowa 51546-0500
Phone: 1-800-831-4190
Fax: 1-800-543-2745
perfectionlearning.com

1 2 3 4 5 6 PP 11 10 09 08 07 06

Paperback ISBN 0-7891-6813-8
Reinforced Library Binding ISBN 0-7569-6348-6

CONTENTS

CHAPTER 1

Left Out

Inch and Miles stood at the edge of the soccer field. The soccer captains had just chosen their teams. Another game was starting—without them.

"Inch, you just don't work hard enough," said Captain Bertha. "You let the other team run all over you."

"Same with you, Miles," Captain Zero said. "You could be a good player if you'd make the effort."

"Yeah," said Bertha. "You're both just too lazy.

Sorry, guys. Show me some sweat and muscle next time if you want to be on the team."

Bertha and Zero jogged out to join their teams on the field. Inch and Miles watched them go. Would they ever get to play?

"Hey, boys," their teacher Mr. Wooden called. "Why the sad looks?"

Inch hung his head. "We never get chosen for the team," he said.

"Never?" asked Mr. Wooden.

"Well, once we did. But the captains said we didn't work hard enough."

"Hmmm," said Mr. Wooden, rubbing his chin. "Miles, I've seen you run. You're a natural. And Inch, your flexibility should take you far. You both should be playing on the team. Have you forgotten the fifteen blocks on my Pyramid of Success—the ones that will help you be your personal best?"

Miles stared at his sneakers. "I remember going on a magical journey and meeting lots of friends—Axelrod, Rhonda, Charlie . . ."

Inch wiggled nervously. "Fourteen friends in all! They gave us clues about the Pyramid of Success . . . but I guess we forgot."

As Inch raised his eyes, he spotted the whistle that hung on a cord around Mr. Wooden's neck. The magic silver whistle! "May we borrow your silver whistle again?" Inch asked.

"Good idea!" said Miles. "It helped us before. Maybe it will help us again."

"I don't know, boys. It doesn't look like it did much good last time."

"Please!" Inch and Miles said together.

"This time will be different. We really want to learn how to be our personal best," said Inch.

"We really want to make the effort," said Miles.

Mr. Wooden rubbed his chin again. "Well, I

do hate seeing you two sitting on the sidelines with such mopey faces. And I do believe in second chances. Maybe the whistle will help. But I have to warn you. Be careful with it—very careful. This whistle cannot be replaced."

"Yes, sir. We'll be careful," Inch said.

"Very careful," Miles added.

Mr. Wooden took the whistle from around his neck and put it on Miles. He had to loop the cord three times to keep the whistle from dragging on the ground.

Miles lifted the whistle to his mouth.

"No, not here," Mr. Wooden said. "Take it to the edge of the school yard. And make sure to pay close attention!"

CHAPTER 2

Life and Death

When Inch and Miles reached the edge of the school yard, Miles blew the whistle. Hootie-toot-toot! The school yard and the noise from the soccer game suddenly disappeared. Inch and Miles floated through creamy cotton clouds. They heard strange sounds like thunder in a bottle, rain in a teakettle, and lightning cracking upside down and sideways. They closed their eyes and plugged their ears. When they opened their eyes again, they were in a new world. One that looked strange and familiar at the same time.

"Hey! It's you two again!" said a small voice from the ground.

Inch and Miles looked down to spy Axelrod the Ant. He was wearing a soccer jersey! Axelrod was a friend they had met on their very first adventure with the magic silver whistle.

"Hey, Axelrod, buddy!" Miles said. "Good to see you again!"

"Yeah," said Inch. "We need your advice. Can you help us learn to work harder?"

"We never get chosen for the soccer team," said Miles. "The captains say we don't make the effort."

"It's depressing," said Inch.

"I'll say it is," said Axelrod. "I remember those days. Nobody chose me either."

"Really?" Miles asked. "So how did you finally make a team?"

"It's a long story," said Axelrod. "I'd love to tell you, but I just can't right now. I've got a big problem of my own—a huge problem!"

"Your problem couldn't be as big as ours!" Inch said.

"That's right," said Miles. "It couldn't be!"

Axelrod shook his head. "Boys, you've got a problem, but I've got a situation. A life-and-death one!"

Inch and Miles looked at each other. "Life and death?" they both said together.

"One of the pupas was stolen from the nursery a few minutes ago. The one that will be the next queen!"

"What's a pupa?" Miles asked.

"It's like a cocoon," Inch told Miles. "You know, where the caterpillar changes into a butterfly?"

"Oh, sure," Miles said. "But why is that your problem, I mean situation?"

"I was in charge of the nursery when it was stolen," Axelrod admitted.

"Uh-oh," said Miles. "That's bad."

"Yeah. That's really, really bad," said Inch.

"I was dead tired last night," Axelrod explained. "Our team, the Movers, had just finished practicing for a soccer tournament. I had worked hard—really, really hard—because I want to be the best player I can for our team. Afterward, it was my turn to watch the nursery.

I fell asleep. When I woke up, the pupa was gone! A slave-maker ant took it. I'm sure."

"Yikes!" Miles said.

"Yikes!" said Inch. "What's a slave-maker ant?"

"An ant that steals pupas for its own colony," Axelrod told them.

"Uh-oh," said Miles. "Slave-maker ants sound dangerous."

"And scary," Inch added. "What are you going to do?"

"I have to get it back. If I don't, our colony won't have a new queen. I know where the slave-makers' dugout is, but it has so many tunnels and rooms. I'm afraid it's too big a task for one small ant." Axelrod hung his head.

"I have an idea," Miles said. "We'll help you find the pupa. Then you'll have time to help us out."

Inch poked Miles and frowned. He didn't like the sound of this plan. It could be dangerous.

"Really?" Axelrod said. "You guys will help me get it back?"

"Sure. Then you'll have time to help us learn to work harder," Miles said.

Inch poked Miles again. "Uh . . .uh . . . I don't know. It sounds too hard . . . too dangerous," Inch said.

"Oh, come on, Inch. We've got to do this . . . for Axelrod."

Miles twirled the silver whistle and winked at Inch.

Inch swallowed hard. Maybe Miles was right. They could use the magic whistle to help them! "Okay," Inch said.

"Deal!" said Axelrod.

"Done deal," said Miles. Miles elbowed Inch.

"Done deal," said Inch.

CHAPTER 3

Big Trouble

"We must get going!" said Axelrod. "There's no time to lose. The princess ant has to hatch inside the ant colony. The first face she sees must belong to the queen mother. If not, the princess ant will die. And if she dies, we won't have a new queen. We must find the pupa before the princess hatches somewhere else. We must bring her back to the colony!"

"So, let's go!" said Miles. He was off and running.

"Wait!" Inch said. "There's a small problem. Actually, it's a *big* problem. We're too big to fit into the ant tunnels."

Miles turned around. "Right," he said, "but the silver whistle can help!"

Miles gave the silver whistle a loud hootie-toot-toot! Inch and Miles found themselves standing next to a huge gleaming object. It was the silver whistle! He and Miles had shrunk, but the whistle hadn't. The whistle was so big that Inch could crawl inside. No way could Miles blow it now!

"Uh-oh," Inch whispered to Miles. "How can we help Axelrod without the silver whistle? How will we get to our normal size and back to school?"

"What's the matter, guys?" Axelrod asked.

"Oh, nothing," said Miles.

"Nothing?" Inch squeaked. He was feeling very, very scared. He was used to being the smallest guy on the playground. But now he was practically ant-sized. He WAS ant-sized! And it looked like he might stay that way forever. Now he would never, ever make the team. Worse, what if the slave-maker ant captured him and made him a slave? His mother would be really, really mad at him!

Before Inch could spend any more time worrying and feeling sorry for himself, Axelrod said, "We've got to hurry, guys. There's something I forgot to tell you. We need to find the pupa before noon tomorrow. That's when the pupa will be brought before the queen to hatch."

"Let's go," said Miles, running ahead. "No time to waste!"

"But where?" asked Inch. He took a deep breath.

"You'll see. Follow me!" said Axelrod.

Miles started to race off with Axelrod, but Inch yelled, "Wait! We need to think about this!"

Miles and Axelrod stopped so Inch could catch up.

"We need to use our heads," Inch told Miles and Axelrod. Maybe he wasn't the bravest or the fastest guy on the planet, but he wasn't stupid.

"What does the pupa look like?" he asked Axelrod.

Axelrod drew a picture in the dirt with a tiny stick.

"That looks like a jelly bean," Inch said. "What color is it?"

"How will we know it when we find it?" Inch asked.

"It will smell like sweet orange blossoms," said Axelrod.

"Sounds like a lot of hard work finding that pupa," Miles said.

"And scary and dangerous," Inch reminded him.

CHAPTER 4

Going It Alone

Inch and Miles followed Axelrod for what seemed like a really long time. They climbed up hills and down, under leaves, and through grass and twigs. Inch stretched and bent his body to crawl over stones. He wanted to rest, but Axelrod kept pushing ahead with Miles right behind him. Inch wished he could move as fast as Miles.

"Ouch!" Axelrod yelled, hopping on one leg.

"What's the matter?" Miles asked.

"I must have tripped over a stone. It's my bad leg . . . an old soccer injury." Axelrod looked like he might cry. "I can't go any farther. Now our colony won't have a new queen, and it will be all my fault!"

"We won't let that happen," Miles said. "We'll find that pupa for you. Right, Inch?"

"Ah . . . ah . . ." Inch stuttered. Miles poked him. "I guess so."

"Good, let's go!" Miles said.

"Wait!" Inch yelled. "We don't know where the slave-makers' dugout is."

Axelrod leaned into a dandelion petal, rubbing his sore leg. "Sorry, guys. This sounds too hard. Maybe you should just quit."

"No," said Miles. "We made a deal, and we're not going back on it. Right, Inch?"

"Right," Inch said, even though he wanted to say "wrong."

"You guys are really true friends," said Axelrod. "But Inch is right. You need more information. See over there?"

Inch and Miles looked to where Axelrod was pointing. A giant fir tree poked up into the sky.

"I'm pretty sure the dugout is just ahead, a little to the right near that fir tree," Axelrod said. "You'll know it's the right dugout when you see a mound of soil and twigs around the opening. Oh, and you can't miss the smell—kind of like dirty socks after a soccer game."

"Yuck," said Inch. He was glad Miles was the one with the good nose. He hated the smell of stinky socks. Gross!

"We can do it," Miles said. "My eyesight's not all that great, but Inch's is. And I've got a great sniffer. Right, Inch?"

"Right," said Inch.

"It will be hard work," Axelrod said, "going through all the tunnels and mazes to find the pupa. You may even have to do some digging of your own."

"That's okay," Miles said. "Inch and I both are great diggers. And Inch is good at stretching and reaching. Right, Inch?"

Inch sighed. "Right."

"One more thing," Axelrod said. "The slave-maker ants leave the dugout at sunrise and return at sunset. But . . ." Axelrod stopped to rub his sore leg. "Be on the lookout for the slave-maker captain. He could return at any time."

Yikes! thought Inch.

CHAPTER 5

Slave-Maker

"I can smell the dugout!" Miles yelled. "Just up ahead."

Inch scurried after Miles, keeping his eyes open for a slave-maker ant. His skin felt sweaty from trying to keep up with Miles.

"This is it!" Miles waved at Inch. "We found it!" Miles ducked into the hole before Inch could yell, "Wait!"

Inch followed Miles into the tunnel.

It was very dark inside, and smelly, even for Inch, whose sniffer wasn't all that great. Axelrod

was right. Stinky socks! Yuck.

"Hurry, Inch!" Miles called.

Inch hurried to catch up. He bent and stretched through the tight tunnels, hoping not to lose sight of Miles. When he finally reached his friend, Inch whispered, "Don't talk so loud! A slave-maker ant might hear us. Remember what Axelrod said about the slave-maker captain? He might come back anytime!"

"You're right," Miles said. "We need to work fast. There are a gazillion tunnels here. Lead the way, buddy. You're the one with the great eyes. I'll keep my sniffer alert for two smells— the slave-maker captain, extremely stinky socks, and the queen-to-be, sweet orange blossoms."

Inch led the way through tunnel after dark tunnel. Some led nowhere, and the two friends were forced to turn back. Some led to rooms with stored food. Inch's stomach growled. But there was no time to stop and eat. He kept pressing forward through the narrow, dark tunnels in search of the pupa that held the next queen. Inch worried that they would never find the pupa in time, no matter how hard they worked.

"Hold on!" Miles said. "I smell something. And it isn't sweet orange blossoms! Dig, Inch, dig! We've got to hide. It's the captain. And he's close!"

Inch dug furiously into the earth. Miles dug too—hard and fast. They dug until they were buried inside a tiny cave of dirt. Inch couldn't see anything. He couldn't even see Miles, but he could feel his warm body next to him. Inch wondered if Miles could feel him shaking. Could Miles smell the slave-maker captain coming closer? Inch was afraid to ask. The ant might hear him.

Miles put his arm around Inch. Inch knew the slave-maker captain was very near, just above them. Even Inch could smell the ant now. He sniffed hard and got a whiff of a whole locker room full of stinking socks! Whew!

Inch trembled harder. What if the slave-maker ant found them? He didn't want to be a slave!

CHAPTER 6

Lost

Inch and Miles waited for what seemed like forever, huddled together in the moist, black earth. Cautiously, Miles whispered, "I think he's gone. I don't smell stinky socks anymore."

"Are you sure?" Inch asked.

"Yup. Unless my sniffer's broken. Let's go, Inch. We've lost a lot of time."

Inch wasn't so sure he wanted to go, but Miles had already started digging.

"Come on, Inch, dig. We need to find the tunnel and continue searching before it's too late to save the pupa."

Inch helped Miles dig. They dug and dug, but they couldn't find the tunnel. They were making a tunnel of their own through the dirt. But where was it leading them? Deeper into the earth or out?

"I think we're lost, Inch," Miles said with a sigh.

"Don't say that. It scares me," Inch said.

"Sorry, buddy. The truth sometimes is scary."

"What can we do?" Inch asked.

"Just keep on digging and hope we get lucky!" Miles answered.

So that's just what Inch and Miles did. Dig, dig, dig, and dig some more. It was hard, hard work moving all that dirt, going around rocks, sticks, and pebbles.

"I've got to rest," Inch said. "I've never worked so hard in my life."

"Me, either," said Miles. "But we can't stop now. We just can't."

So Inch kept digging with all the might he could muster.

"Hold it!" said Miles. "I smell something!"

"Stinky socks?"

"No, sweet orange blossoms! Keep digging. We're close!"

Inch burrowed through the earth in front of him. The next thing he knew he was in a tiny room. A bit of light filtered in, enough so that he could see. There in the corner was a cream-colored jelly bean—the pupa! Even he could smell the sweet scent of orange blossoms.

"Miles, come quick!" he yelled. "I think I found it. The future queen!"

"You're right! Orange blossoms. Most

definitely. Good going, buddy." Miles gently lifted the pupa. He tucked it, football-style, close to his body. "Let's go!"

Ahead, they saw an ant tunnel that led out of the room. Now all they had to do was follow the tunnel and they would be out. They would find Axelrod. He would take the pupa to the queen! That is IF they didn't run into the captain slave-maker or other slave-makers! IF they could get out in time. IF!

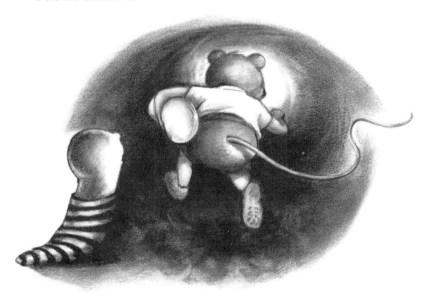

CHAPTER 7

Trapped!

Miles started into the tunnel that led out of the room. "Wait a sec," Inch said. "There's a bit of light in this room. That means we're not too far down. Maybe we could dig our own way out, starting here." Inch pointed up.

"Hmm. Not a bad idea, Inch. But it will take more hard work. Uh-oh!" Miles said.

"What's the matter?"

"Stinky socks! Lots of them! It must be sundown. The slave-makers are returning!"

"What are we going to do?" The moment

Inch said those words, he felt dirt fall on his head. The ground below and above shook. Dirt was falling everywhere.

"Cave-in!" yelled Miles.

The earth shook and shook. Inch wondered if he would ever see his mother again. He was being buried alive!

Finally, the shaking stopped. But Inch was up to his eyeballs in dirt.

"Can you breathe?" Miles asked Inch. Only his eyes and nose stuck out of the dirt.

"Yes," Inch whispered. "What happened?"

"I don't know. It felt like an earthquake. Maybe an animal or human stepped on the dugout. Hard to know."

"What about the slave-makers?" Inch asked. "Do you smell anything?"

"No. Maybe they were killed. Or maybe they left."

"What about the pupa?" Inch asked.

"I still have it. It's safe. But wait!" Miles said. "I feel something. Something moving inside the pupa!"

"Uh-oh!" said Inch. "Maybe it's hatching!"

"I think you're right! You heard what Axelrod said. If it hatches away from home, if it doesn't see the queen mother, it will die! We gotta get it out of here. Quick."

Inch wiggled his way loose from the dirt.

Then he pushed the dirt away from Miles, who held the pupa tight.

"Thanks, Inch," Miles said. "Now more digging . . . straight up this time."

"Up and out!" said Inch.

"Up and out!" said Miles.

With all his strength, Inch burrowed and dug a tunnel toward the light. Miles, holding the pupa tight, followed after him. At last Inch broke through. He took a deep breath of fresh air. It hadn't been easy, but at last they were above the earth, not under it.

"Yes!" Inch said, but not too loudly. He didn't want any slave-maker to hear.

Miles, still holding the pupa and covered in dirt, crawled out after Inch.

Inch shook himself. Dirt flew everywhere! He knew his mother would have a fit when she saw his ears!

Miles gently set the pupa down and brushed off the dirt that clung to him, from the top of his head to his toes. "Now, let's find Axelrod!"

"I can't," Inch said. "I'm too tired. I've got to rest."

"No time," Miles said. "This little princess wants to hatch."

Miles started to race off.

"Wait!" Inch called. "We need a plan. We need to think."

Miles stopped and hurried back to Inch.

"Okay. What's the plan?"

"The fir tree. We left Axelrod south of it. Remember?"

Miles stuck his nose in the air and sniffed hard. "There!" he said, pointing west. "I can smell it!"

"And south is this way," Inch said. "You can tell by the sun. Let's go!"

CHAPTER 8

Hard Work

Inch scurried south as fast as he could to where he hoped Axelrod would be waiting, but Miles raced ahead.

When Inch finally caught up with Miles, he was too tired to move another half inch. That's when he spotted Axelrod crawling out from under a leaf. "Axelrod!" he called.

Axelrod waved at Inch and Miles as he hobbled toward them. "You got it! You got it!" Axelrod shouted. His face was one big grin.

"Now we have to get you and this pupa back

to the ant colony," Miles said. "She's ready to hatch."

Axelrod's smile turned to a frown. "You and Inch will have to go without me. I can't walk fast enough."

"I have a plan," Inch said. "We'll make a stretcher and carry you on it!"

"Great idea, Inch," Miles said.

Making a stretcher out of a leaf, grass strands, and twigs was no easy task for Inch and Miles. When Axelrod was safely on the stretcher, Miles handed him the pupa. "Hold on tight, buddy," he told Axelrod.

Together, the three friends began their journey back to the ant colony with the future queen.

When they reached the edge of the ant colony, Axelrod said, "Let me down, guys. I've got to go it alone now."

"Inch and Miles lowered the stretcher, and Axelrod crawled off, holding the pupa tightly.

"I can feel the princess ant moving inside the pupa!" Axelrod said. "Got to hurry!"

"Good luck!" Inch and Miles both said.

Axelrod, trying hard not to limp, walked toward the anthole that led to the queen's chambers.

Inch and Miles crawled under a leaf. They were dead tired from all the work they'd done. Soon they were sound, sound asleep.

✿ ✿

"Ouch!" Inch said. He felt a poke. He opened one eye. Axelrod was standing there smiling at him.

"You saved my life, guys. Saved the colony. How can I ever repay you?"

"You said you'd help us with our problem," Miles said, stretching.

Inch stretched too. His muscles ached from the digging, climbing, and hurrying from the day before. But it was a good ache.

"Oh, yes. Now what was your problem?" Axelrod asked.

For a moment, Inch and Miles couldn't remember what their problem was!

Then Miles said, "Now I remember! We never get chosen for the soccer team. The captains say we don't know how to work hard. That we don't put forth the effort."

Axelrod laughed. "I think you've solved your

problem yourselves. Friends, I've never seen anyone work harder than you two! You saved my job, my life, and the future of this colony! If you work half that hard playing soccer, no one will ever question your effort again. Guaranteed!"

Inch and Miles looked at each other. Maybe Axelrod was right! They had given 100 percent effort and worked harder than they could ever remember working.

Axelrod handed Miles a small card. "Here's my card. If you ever need anything, give a holler."

"Well," said Inch, "we need something right now. We need to get back to school. We need to give our teacher his whistle!" He looked at the giant silver whistle. "But how can we? We're too small to blow the magic whistle!"

"Hard work, that's how," said Axelrod. "The three of us together blowing hard can make a mighty wind."

"Let's do it!" said Miles.

And they did. Together the three friends blew with all their strength into the gigantic silver whistle, enough to make a mighty wind, enough to make the magic work. Suddenly Inch and Miles were floating through creamy cotton clouds. They heard strange sounds like thunder in a bottle, rain in a teakettle, and lightning cracking upside down and sideways.

They closed their eyes and plugged their ears. When they opened their eyes again, they were standing in the school yard, right next to their teacher!

"So boys, I see you're back . . . with my silver whistle." Mr. Wooden smiled. "So how was my friend Axelrod? Was he able to stop working long enough to offer some advice?"

Before Inch or Miles could tell Mr. Wooden about their hard work helping Axelrod save the princess pupa and the ant colony, Zero and Bertha ran up.

"How'd the game go?" Mr. Wooden asked the two captains.

"We lost," Zero said. "The team just didn't work hard enough!"

Miles laughed. "Well, if you'll let Inch and me play tomorrow, we'll show you what hard work looks like." He ran in place a bit to show off his leg muscles.

"Yeah," agreed Inch, wiping the sweat from his brow.

Zero elbowed Bertha. "Well, well—sweat and muscle. Sure, we could use a good runner and a new goalie. Play tomorrow and show us how hard you can work!"

Inch and Miles looked at each other and smiled. They had learned all about hard work and how it could pay off. If they could save an entire ant colony with hard work, they knew they could help the team win tomorrow. The two friends high-fived, then fell over, exhausted.

Axelrod the Ant

I may be small. That's very true.
But I Succeed, and so can you.
I move a mountain, bit by bit.
It takes Hard Work—I never sit.
I Work and Work throughout the day.
My Work comes first before I play.
Success is yours, please understand,
When you and Work go hand in hand.

ABOUT THE AUTHORS

Coach and teacher **John Wooden** is a towering figure in 20th-century American sports. His UCLA basketball teams virtually created "March Madness" by amassing 10 national championships, 7 in a row; along with 4 perfect seasons; an 88-game winning streak; and 38 straight victories in tournament play.

Sports Illustrated says, "There has never been a finer man in American sports, or a finer coach."

Coach Wooden has two children, seven grandchildren, and eleven great-grandchildren.
(Visit CoachJohnWooden.com)

Steve Jamison is a best-selling author, award-winning television producer, and public speaker.
(Visit SteveJamison.com)

Bonnie Graves is the author of 13 books for young readers, both fiction and nonfiction. Beginning with *The Best Worst Day* in 1996, she has received several awards and honors for her work, including a 2005 South Carolina Children's Book Award nomination for her chapter book *Taking Care of Trouble*.